Text copyright © 2007 by Miles Backer

Pictures copyright © 2007 by Chuck Nitzberg

All rights reserved

CIP Data is available.

Published in the United States 2007 by

🍎 Blue Apple Books

P.O. Box 1380, Maplewood, N.J. 07040

www.blueapplebooks.com

Distributed in the U.S. by Chronicle Books

First Edition

Printed in China

ISBN 10: 1-59354-594-0

ISBN 13: 978-1-59354-594-9

1 3 5 7 9 10 8 6 4 2

TRAVELS with CHARLIE

Down SOUTH

Miles Backer

Illustrated by Chuck Nitzberg

 BLUE APPLE BOOKS

You'll travel the Mississippi
on an old riverboat.

You'll see water skiers
on big Lake Chicot.

You'll spot Mount Vernon,
George Washington's home,
And stop in the Everglades
where alligators roam.

You'll see Graceland,

the home of Elvis "The King."

You'll find the Louisville Slugger

and the World Peace Bell to ring.

There's lots of racetracks

for horses and cars,

And the Kennedy Space Center

where they shoot for the stars.

If you follow Charlie

from state to state,

you'll see the whole South.

Now, won't that be great?

Alabama *The Cotton State*

Where's the U.S. Space and Rocket Center?

Where's the Cumberland Plateau?

Where's the Civil Rights Trail?

Where did Rosa Parks say no?

Find the Chattahoochee River.

Find the Peanut Queen.

Find Hellen Keller's home

At Ivy Green.

Where's Charlie?

U.S. SPACE AND ROCKET CENTER

TENNESSEE RIVER

Huntsville

CUMBERLAND PLATEAU

WATER!

Ivy Green

Vulcan THE IRON MAN

Birmingham

LOST TRAIL MAZE

Tuscaloosa

CIVIL RIGHTS MARCH NATIONAL HISTORIC TRAIL

DeSoto Caverns

SHORTER MANSION

Rosa Parks Museum

Selma   Montgomery

MOUNDSVILLE ARCHAEOLOGICAL PARK AND NATIVE AMERICAN FESTIVAL

FENDALL HALL

Miss National Peanut Queen Pageant

CHATTAHOOCHEE RIVER

THE TAVERN

BELLINGRATH GARDENS AND HOME

Dothan

Mobile

U.S.S. ALABAMA BATTLESHIP MEMORIAL PARK

FORT MORGAN

EUFAULA PILGRIMAGE

Arkansas

The Natural State

Where's a place to look for diamonds?

Where's a concert that rocks?

Where's a haven for elephants?

Where do turkeys trot?

Find the boggy creek monster.

Find watermelon in Hope.

Find the Mississippi River.

Find Lake Chicot.

Where's Charlie?

Ozark Mountains

Turkey Trot Festival

Cotter

Yellville

Wilson

Fort Smith

Fort Smith Symphony Annual Earthquake Concert

Greenbrier

Hampson Archaeological Museum State Park

Clinton Presidential Center

Little Rock

Hot Springs

White Water River

Murfreesboro Crater of Diamonds State Park

Rohwer

Hope

Japanese-American Internment Camp Marker

Mississippi River

Lake Chicot

Boggy Creek Monster

Florida
The Sunshine State

Where's Cape Canaveral?

Where do oranges grow?

Where are the Everglades?

Where does the Suwannee flow?

Find a pirate museum.

Look for Key West.

Then find Miami

Where the beach is the best.

Where's Charlie?

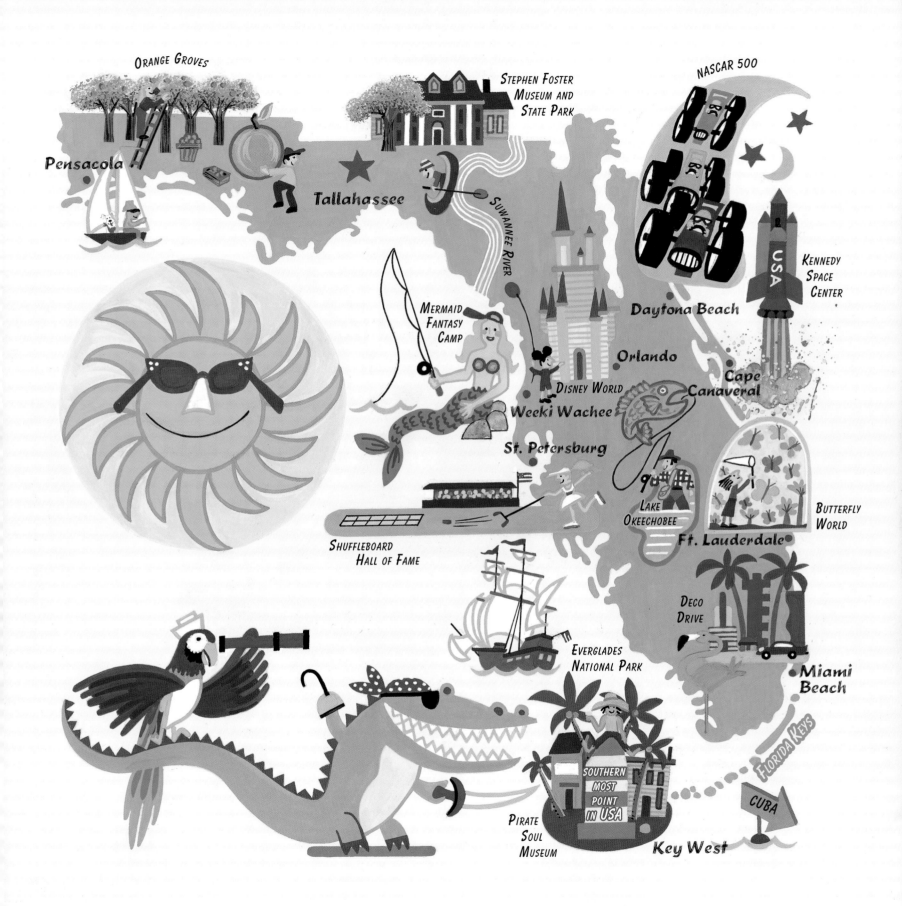

Orange Groves

Stephen Foster Museum and State Park

NASCAR 500

Pensacola

Tallahassee

Suwannee River

Kennedy Space Center

USA

Mermaid Fantasy Camp

Daytona Beach

Orlando

Cape Canaveral

Disney World

Weeki Wachee

St. Petersburg

Lake Okeechobee

Butterfly World

Shuffleboard Hall of Fame

Ft. Lauderdale

Deco Drive

Everglades National Park

Miami Beach

Florida Keys

Pirate Soul Museum

SOUTHERN MOST POINT IN USA

Key West

CUBA

Georgia
The Peach State

Where's the Okefenokee Swamp?

Where's a place to pick a peach?

Can you find a big cake,

And Jekyll Island by the beach?

Find a huge smiling peanut.

Trace Sherman's march to the sea.

Find the homes of old Savannah

And a place to sleep in a tree!

Where's Charlie?

BLUE RIDGE MOUNTAINS

Chickamauga

Coke

SHERMAN'S
MARCH TO THE SEA

Athens

TREE THAT
OWNS ITSELF

Atlanta

CLARK HILL
LAKE

Augusta

DAVENPORT HOUSE

JULIETTE
GORDON
LOW
BIRTHPLACE

MARTIN LUTHER KING,
JR., NATIONAL
HISTORIC SITE

OWENS THOMAS HOUSE

PEACH
PICKIN'
ORCHARD

SMILING
PEANUT

OCMULGEE
INDIAN NATIONAL
MONUMENT

Claxton

HISTORIC
DISTRICT

Savannah

CHATTAHOOCHEE RIVER

LAKE
SEMINOLE

TREE HOUSE HOSTEL

Jekyll
Island

OKEFENOKEE SWAMP

Kentucky *The Bluegrass State*

Where's Mammoth Cave?

Where's the World Peace Bell?

Where is the forest

Daniel Boone knew so well?

Find the Cumberland Falls.

Find a big baseball bat.

Find Churchill Downs,

And a cow in a hat.

Where's Charlie?

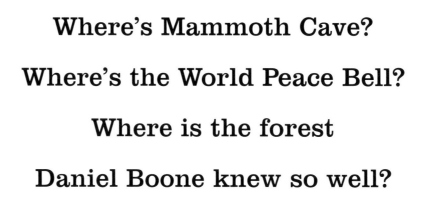

CHURCHILL DOWNS

KENTUCKY DERBY

FINISH

Charlie

WORLD PEACE BELL

Newport

LOUISVILLE SLUGGER MUSEUM

DANIEL BOONE NATIONAL FOREST

OWENSBORO BBQ FESTIVAL

Louisville

Fort Knox

Frankfort

MISSISSIPPI RIVER

Paducah

Hodgenville

New Haven

LAKE CUMBERLAND

MOONBOW

WIGWAM VILLAGE

L&N STEAM LOCOMOTIVE

MAMMOTH CAVE

CUMBERLAND FALLS

Louisiana *The Bayou State*

Where's Audubon Park?

Where is Tabasco sauce made?

Where's Lake Calcasieu?

Where's a Mardi Gras parade?

Find the Atchafalaya Swamp.

Find a wild crawfish boil.

Find an offshore rig

Where they drill for oil.

Where's Charlie?

LOUISIANA PURCHASE GARDENS AND ZOO

Shreveport

Monroe

MELROSE PLANTATION

MUDBUG MADNESS CRAWFISH BOIL

ATCHAFALAYA SWAMP

Mississippi River

AUDUBON MEMORIAL STATE PARK

SHRIMP CREOLE

Baton Rouge

SABINE RIVER

FROG CAPITAL OF THE WORLD

TABASCO FACTORY TOUR

LAKE PONTCHARTRAIN CAUSEWAY

Lake Pontchartrain

New Orleans

Lake Calcasieu

Avery Island

Rayne

SAINT LOUIS CATHEDRAL

BOURBON ST.

OFFSHORE OIL RIG

FRENCH QUARTER

JACKSON SQUARE

MARDI GRAS

Mississippi

The Hospitality State

DID YOU KNOW...

- In 1902, President Theodore Roosevelt refused to shoot a bear that had been captured during a hunting trip in Sharkey County, MS. This act inspired the creation of the first teddy bear.

- Greenwood, MS, is one of the few places in the world where you can stand between two rivers flowing in opposite directions: the Yalobusha River and the Tallahatchie River.

- The South is sprinkled with antebellum mansions that date back to before the Civil War. Natchez, MS, features more than thirty of these grand homes.

- Vicksburg is the site of the Civil War battle that gave the North control of the Mississippi River. After a battle that lasted almost two months, the Confederacy surrendered Vicksburg to the Union.

Where's a Petrified Forest?

Where does cotton grow?

Where's a Mississippi riverboat?

Where's a herd of buffalo?

Find the battlefield at Vicksburg.

Find a dance competition.

Find a place to play checkers

And a spot for shrimp fishin'.

Where's Charlie?

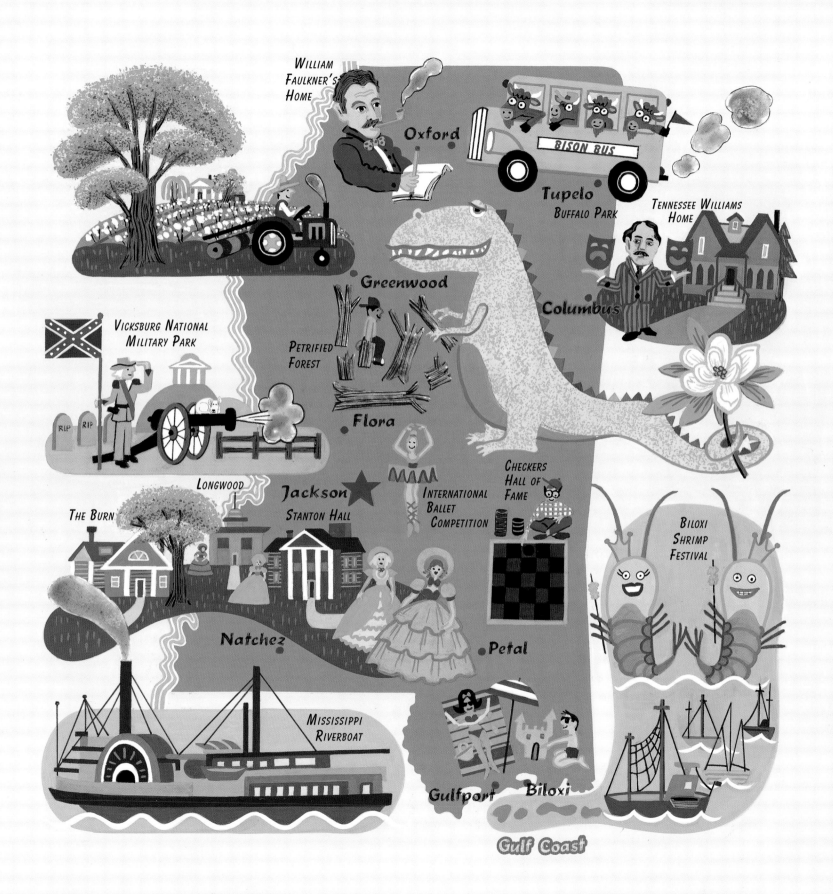

North Carolina

The Tar Heel State

Where's the Biltmore Mansion?

Where's the Cape Hatteras Light?

Where's the place where the Wright brothers made the first flight?

Find the Alphabet Museum.

Find Blackbeard's domain.

Find a health center

Where you can stroll through a brain.

Where's Charlie?

South Carolina

The Palmetto State

Where's a ginkgo tree farm?

Where's Myrtle Beach?

Where's Raven Cliff Falls?

Where's a giant peach?

Find Sheldon and Salley.

Find the village Oyotunji.

Find two dancing pigs,

And an old cypress tree.

Where's Charlie?

Tennessee

The Volunteer State

Where was Davey Crockett born?

Where do country bands sing?

Where's Elvis's home?

Where do airplanes take wing?

Find Ruby Falls Cavern.

Find a Mule Day Queen.

Find the steepest railroad

you've ever seen.

Where's Charlie?

Skyblazers Air Park

Grand Ole Opry

Grand Guitar Music Museum

Davey Crockett Birthplace

Bristol

Mississippi River

Tennessee River

Nashville

Columbia

Jonesboro

Knoxville

Appalachian Mountains

Shiloh Military Park

Futuro Flying Saucer House

Memphis

Shiloh

Chattanooga

Graceland

Incline Railroad

Lookout Mountain

Lost Sea Cavern

Ruby Falls Cavern

Tennessee Civil War Museum

Virginia *Old Dominion*

DID YOU KNOW . . .

- English explorers founded the first permanent European settlement in North America at Jamestown, VA, in 1607.

- Richmond was the capital of the Confederacy during the Civil War.

- Eight United States presidents were born in Virginia: George Washington, Thomas Jefferson, James Madison, James Monroe, William Henry Harrison, John Tyler, Zachary Taylor, and Woodrow Wilson.

- Every year the wild ponies of Assateague Island are brought across the Assateague Channel to be sold on Chincoteague Island. At one time, the ponies were brought over by boat, but in 1924 the handlers chose to swim them across the channel, and they have done so ever since.

Where's Chincoteague Island?

Where do knights joust?

Where's Monticello,

Thomas Jefferson's house?

Find Colonial Williamsburg.

Find a hot air balloon.

Find a music museum

Where country stars croon.

Where's Charlie?

SHENANDOAH VALLEY
HOT AIR BALLOON FESTIVAL

APPLE BLOSSOM FESTIVAL

CHINCOTEAGUE
PONY PENNING

NATIONAL JOUSTING
HALL OF FAME

Monticello

Mt. Vernon

Appomattox
Courthouse

Richmond

Yogaville
Williamsburg

CHINCOTEAGUE
ISLAND

APPALACHIAN MOUNTAINS

COUNTRY MUSIC
MUSEUM

Bristol

KEEP ON
THE
SUNNY
SIDE

CARTER FAMILY BIRTHPLACE AND MUSEUM

COLONIAL
WILLIAMSBURG

West Virginia *The Mountain State*

Did You Know . . .

- West Virginia broke away from Virginia during the Civil War, and is the only state to have been formed by a Presidential Proclamation.

- West Virginia's network of rivers and railroads, as well as its natural resources of silica sand and stone, have led to the creation of more than 500 glass factories.

- With a 1,700-foot span, the New River Gorge Bridge is the second longest steel arch bridge in the world.

- Coal can be found in 53 of 55 counties in West Virginia and is one of the state's largest industries.

- In 1859, John Brown led a small group of followers in a raid on the Arsenal at Harpers Ferry in the hopes of gathering weapons to support a slave uprising in the South. Brown was captured and executed but served as inspiration for other abolitionists.

Where's Snowshoe Mountain?

Where is glass made?

Where's Harpers Ferry,

Site of John Brown's raid?

Find New River Gorge Bridge.

Find a white water raft.

Find the Cass Scenic Railroad

And a coal mine shaft.

Where's Charlie?

West Virginia
Penitentiary Tour

Chester

World's
Largest
Teapot

Wheeling

Moundsville

Glass
Festival

John
Brown

Potomac River

Mothman
Festival

Stonewall Jackson
Birthplace

Clarksburg

Harpers
Ferry

National
Radio
Astronomy
Observatory

Point Pleasant

Ohio River

Charleston

Green
Bank

Snowshoe
Mountain

Cass Scenic Railroad

New River
Gorge
Bridge

Coal House

Beckley

White Sulphur
Springs

Coal Exhibition

White Water Rafting

Now that you've traveled the South with Charlie,
it's time to earn some extra credit.
There's one riddle for each state. Good luck!

Can You Find . . .

a place in West Virginia
called White Sulphur Springs . . .

an exhibit in Florida
filled with butterfly wings . . .

a maze in Alabama
where it's easy to get lost . . .

the earthquake center in Arkansas
where people get tossed . . .

a place in Georgia
where a famous drink is made . . .

a house in Mississippi
where a great playwright stayed . . .

teepees in Kentucky

near the Mammoth Caves . . .

Surf City, North Carolina,

where surfers catch big waves . . .

a boat in South Carolina

where airplanes land . . .

a festival in Virgina

with a big, brass band . . .

a Tennessee museum

all about guitars . . .

a place in Louisiana

where frogs are the stars?

Good
Work!

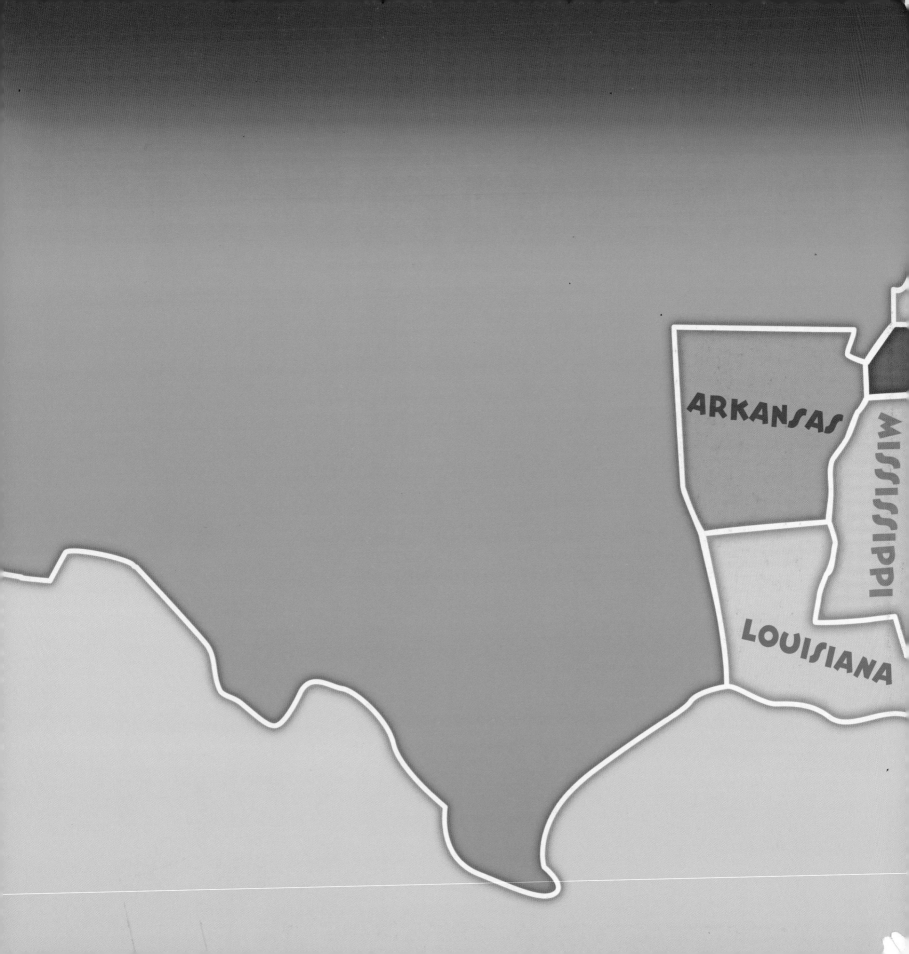